HECTOR'S NEW TRAINERS

For my sisters

First published in Great Britain by
HarperCollins Publishers Ltd in 1993
Text and illustrations copyright © 1993 Amanda Vesey
A CIP catalogue record for this title is available
from the British Library.
The author assert the moral right to be
identified as the author of the work.

Printed and bound in Great Britain
by BPCC Paulton Books Ltd
This book is set in 18/24 Garamond

HECTOR'S NEW TRAINERS

Amanda Vesey

Collins

An Imprint of HarperCollinsPublishers

It was Hector's birthday and there was an exciting parcel waiting for him on the breakfast table.

Hector wanted trainers. He wanted special trainers with go-faster stripes, black and blue trim, cushioned inner soles, padded tongues, a high profile multi-surface tread pattern and a football logo stitched to the ankle collar.

All his friends had trainers like that.

"With the right trainers Leroy might pick me for the team," thought Hector.

Leroy was the school hero: fearless and bold, strong and true, captain of games, winner of sports, champion of the skateboard.

"I hope, I hope," said Hector, tearing off the wrapping paper and opening the box...

"Brilliant!" shouted Hector. He gave his parents a Thank
You hug.

Hector's trainers had go-faster stripes, black and blue trim, cushioned inner soles, padded tongues and a high profile multi-surface tread pattern.

But stitched to the ankle, where there should have been a football, there was a little gold star.

"These look like the right trainers," said Hector. "But they are not the right trainers. They should have a football stitched to the ankle. I wanted the trainers that all my friends have."
He was very disappointed.

"True, they're not quite the same," said Hector's mother.
"They're cheaper. But try them on, they may be more
special than you think. It's nice to be a bit different."

"I like being the same," said Hector.

Hector put on his trainers.

They looked good. They felt fine. But there was no football on the ankle collar.

"They look very sporty," said his father.

"I hope they fit properly," said his mother.

"Do you like my new trainers?" Hector asked his grandmother.

"Not much," said his grandmother. "They make your feet look so big."

"I like big feet," said Hector.

Hector ran into the garden. He bobbed and bounced.
He sprang and pranced. His shoes were so springy he
felt he could run and jump for miles and miles.

THUMP! Hector took a flying leap into the sand pit, landing
on both feet. A perfect set of prints from his high profile
multi-surface tread pattern soles was left in the sand.

He stamped a crazy design of footprints all over the sand pit.

Hector rocked and rolled down to the playground where his friends were kicking a ball.

"WOW! Look at Hector's feet," called Bernadette. "Trendee."

"There's a silly gold star on the ankle where a football ought to be," said Gordon. "Those trainers aren't the real thing."

"They are," said Hector. But he didn't really think so.

Hector plodded sadly home. His feet didn't feel so bouncy any more.

On his way he met some bad boys loafing about on the corner of the street.

"What have we here?" said one of the bad boys. "He's not old enough for trainers like that."

"We could get big money for those trainers," said another. "Lets get him."

Hector tried to run away but the bad boys were too fast. One seized Hector. Another pulled off his trainers. The third kept look out.

"Give me back my trainers!" wept Hector.

But the bad boys just laughed.

WHOOSH!
Round the corner, deftly
weaving his skateboard
down the road, came
Leroy the school hero;
fearless and bold,
strong and true.

With one glance he took in Hector's plight. With a masterly
slappy grind he slid to a stop.

"Hand those trainers back!" thundered Leroy.

He wheelied straight at the bad boys.

"Oi!" "Help!" cried the bad boys, as Leroy aerialed into them. One boy landed in a fruit barrow, another in some rubbish sacks.

"What a mover!" gasped Hector.

Leroy withered the third boy with a look.

"Give him back his trainers!" he commanded. The bad boy shivered and shook. He threw the trainers down in the road.

"They're rubbish trainers anyway," he mumbled as he slunk away.

Hector put on his trainers and Leroy fetched his skateboard.

"Your trainers are cool," said Leroy.

"They're not the real thing," said Hector.

"Not the real thing?" said Leroy. "Says who?"

"They all do," said Hector. But he felt suddenly better.

"Will you come to tea today?" asked Hector. "It's my birthday, and there will be cake."

"Maybe," called Leroy, cruising off.

When Leroy turned up at Hector's birthday party Gordon and
Bernadette were most impressed.

"Lee-roy, Hector's got the wrong kind of trainers," said Bernadette, sucking up.

"That makes two of us!" said Leroy. And they saw that Leroy, the school hero, had brand new trainers with little gold stars on, just the same as Hector's.

Hector and Gordon and Bernadette were stunned.

"I'll swap my trainers for yours, Hector," offered Gordon, "though they're not the real thing."

Hector laughed. He handed round his birthday cake.

"Not the real thing?"

"Says who?" said Hector